For my heroes Lindsey and Kathryn,
with huge admiration and love
xx VF

For Grace, Juliet and Richard,
with love
CF

ORCHARD BOOKS
338 Euston Road, London NW1 3BH
Orchard Books Australia
Level 17/207, Kent Street, Sydney, NSW 2000
First published in Great Britain in 2007
First paperback publication 2008
Text © copyright Vivian French 2007
Illustrations © copyright Chris Fisher 2007
The rights of Vivian French and Chris Fisher to be
identified as the author and illustrator of this work
have been asserted by them in accordance with
the Copyright, Designs and Patents Act, 1988.

A CIP catalogue record for this book is
available from the British Library.

ISBN 978 1 84362 703 6 (hardback)
ISBN 978 1 84362 712 8 (paperback)

1 3 5 7 9 10 8 6 4 2 (hardback)
1 3 5 7 9 10 8 6 4 2 (paperback)
Printed in Great Britain by
Antony Rowe Ltd, Chippenham, Wiltshire

Orchard Books is a division of Hachette Children's Books,
an Hachette Livre UK company.
www.orchardbooks.co.uk

DRAGLINS FIND A HERO!

VIVIAN FRENCH   CHRIS FISHER

ORCHARD BOOKS

CHAPTER ONE

"PHEW!" Dennis said. "It's SO hot! Do you think it'll ever rain again?"

"Dunno," Danny said, and he shifted further into the shade of the ivy. "I'm boiling."

Daffodil never liked to be beaten by anyone. "Bet you're not as hot as I am," she said. "I'm about to burn up into a little crisp!"

"You should move out of the sun," Dora said in disapproving tones. "You'll get your ears burnt."

Daffy made a face. "Don't be so stuffy, Dor."

Dora sighed. Sometimes it was hard being the sensible one. "It's me you'll moan at when you can't get to sleep tonight," she pointed out.

"I NEVER moan!" Daffodil was shocked

at the very idea. "When do I ever moan? Dennis, do I ever moan? Danny, have you ever heard me moan?"

"You're moaning now," Danny told her, and ducked swiftly as Daffodil chucked a handful of dry leaves at his head.

It was the summer holidays, and the four little draglins were sitting on the top of an old water cistern above an abandoned and broken down garden shed. No human beings had been that way for years, which was why the floor of the shed made such an excellent shelter for the draglins' home. And even if a human had fought its way down the old tenement garden, thick with long grass and tangled briars, it would have needed the sharpest of eyes to see the well-disguised front door.

"Dora! Dennis! Daffy! Danny!" It was Aunt Plum, calling from down below. "Time for lunch!"

"Bother," Dennis grumbled. "I wanted another swim."

"Mmmmm!" Danny sniffed the air. "I think it's hazelnut pie!"

"My FAVOURITE!" Daffodil leapt for the ivy.

"And mine," said Dennis.

As the four draglins scrambled downwards, Dennis caught sight of Uncle Damson, Uncle Plant and Uncle Puddle stomping towards the Underground.

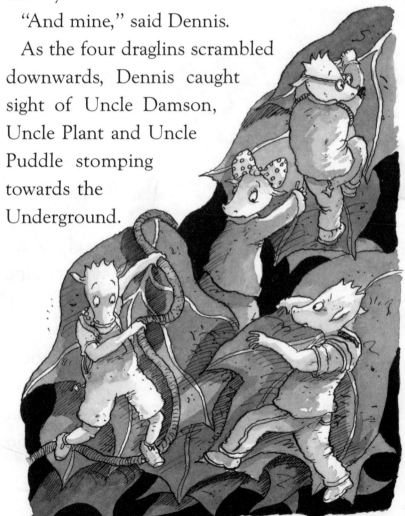

"Wonder where they're off to?" he said. "They look really grim! And Uncle Plant said we weren't to go into the Underground at all today, so how come they can?"

Daffodil shrugged. "They spent all yesterday having gloomy conversations with Aunt Plum, but when I asked what was wrong Uncle Damson said, 'It's nothing a little girlie draglin can do anything about!' HUH!"

"I think it's something to do with the weather," Danny said. "I overheard them talking last night."

"The WEATHER?" Dennis stared at his brother. "What's that got to do with anything?"

Danny shrugged. "Don't ask me. Something about cracks."

Dora's imagination went into immediate overdrive. "CRACKS? Oh NO! Maybe the earth's going to crack open and we'll all fall in and get swallowed up—"

"Shut up, Dor," Danny said, but not unkindly. "Of course it isn't. We'll ask Aunt Plum what's going on over lunch. She'll tell us, if the uncles aren't around."

CHAPTER TWO

Aunt Plum was looking more than usually distracted when the four little draglins came hurrying into the kitchen. She didn't even ask if they'd washed their hands, and Dora's heart sank. There must be something seriously wrong, because Aunt Plum ALWAYS asked. She sat in front of her soup, and couldn't even bring herself to pick up her spoon.

"Dora – what's the matter?" Aunt Plum had finally noticed that Dora wasn't eating. Dennis, Danny and Daffodil had already had two helpings each, and their little cousin Pip was chomping his way through an enormous crust.

"She thinks the earth's going to swallow us up," Daffodil said helpfully, her mouth full of hazelnut pie.

"What?" Aunt Plum was so surprised she

sat down. "Dora, wherever did you get that idea?"

Dora whispered, "Danny said the uncles were looking for cracks..."

"Oh." Aunt Plum was so obviously trying not to smile that Dora began to feel better. "Well, I don't think you'll be falling into any of them." She looked at Daffodil's questioning face. "I suppose I'd better tell you, so you don't all go thinking things are worse than they are."

"Yes PLEASE!" Daffodil beamed at Aunt Plum. "Then we can fix it!"

"That," Aunt Plum told her, "would be beyond even you, Daffodil." She sighed. "It's the Underground. We've always taken our tunnels for granted, but now they're in real danger. It hasn't rained for ages, and the earth's so dry that cracks are appearing in the walls – and in a couple of places the roof's fallen in. That's why the uncles told you to keep away. Of course we've sealed off the tunnels, but if it happens again, and a Beanie notices—" Aunt Plum stopped.

"What would they do?" Dennis was wide-eyed. "What would they do, Aunt Plum?"

Aunt Plum sighed. "Uncle Damson thinks they might dig up the Underground to see where it goes."

Dora gave a loud squeal. "Oh oh OH! They'll dig us up, and we'll be eaten alive!"

"REALLY, Dora!" Aunt Plum frowned. "Don't be so ridiculous! Our home tunnels are quite safe. It's the Underground on the other side of the garden wall that's the problem. It runs under rough grassy ground, and Beanies often walk there."

Danny was looking thoughtful. "Wouldn't they just think it was a wabbit hole?"

"Some of it looks like wabbit tunnels," Aunt Plum agreed. "But – " she hesitated – "there's your school. If the Human Beanies found that, they'd wonder who built it, and what it's for, because Beanies are the nosiest

14

creatures in the world. And the school's in the most dangerous place – that's where the cracks are the worst."

"So what are the uncles doing?" Daffodil wanted to know.

Aunt Plum removed the hazelnut pie out of Daffodil's reach, and sighed again. "They've gone to a meeting to discuss whether the school should be taken down."

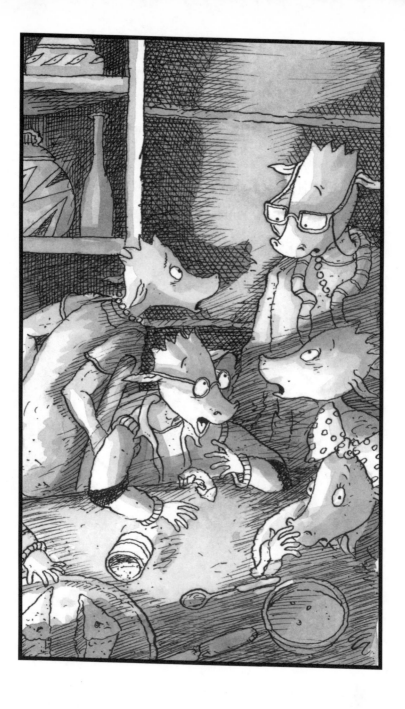

CHAPTER THREE

ennis, Daffodil, Danny and Dora stared at her. For all that they fussed and complained about school, the idea that it might disappear was shocking. School was where they met their friends, and played bootball, and had fun. They even enjoyed some of the lessons, although Daffodil and Dennis would never admit it.

"Take it DOWN?" Dennis said. "Why can't they just hide it?"

"That's right!" Daffodil was up on her feet. "We'll help! We can put stuff over the roof!"

Aunt Plum shook her head. "I don't think that would be enough, Daffodil. But we're probably worrying about nothing. If it rains in the next couple of days everything will be fine."

"Oh." Daffodil looked almost disappointed. "Oh, well. Why can't I have another piece of pie?"

"Because Dora hasn't had any, and you've had three slices," Aunt Plum told her.

"It's all right," Dora said. "She can have mine."

Aunt Plum looked sharply at Dora. "Now, you're not having any more silly ideas, are you?" she asked. "You're quite safe, you know."

"Yes, Aunt Plum," Dora said, but she didn't finish her soup.

After lunch, Aunt Plum sent the four draglins into the storage area behind the shed.

"You can keep an eye on Pip for me," she said firmly. "I'm going to do some washing while the sunshine lasts."

"But—" Daffodil began.

"NO buts." Aunt Plum folded her arms. "It'll do you good to spend some time in the shade. Your ears are bright red!"

Dennis and Danny had been whispering in the corner. "Come on, Daffy," Danny said. "We've had an idea!"

Daffodil brightened, and trotted away, followed by Dora and Pip. As soon as they reached the storage space Dennis lifted Pip into his swing. With a massive push he sent the little draglin soaring up to the roof, shrieking with pleasure.

"That'll keep him happy for a bit," Dennis said. "Now – Danny and I have got a plan!"

Dora's heart sank even further. There was something about Dennis's shining eyes that made her suspect an adventure.

"What is it?" Daffodil demanded. "What sort of a plan?"

Dennis grinned. "We're going to go and look at the cracks," he announced. "Whatever Aunt Plum says, I bet we can think of something!"

"We're bound to meet the uncles," Daffodil objected.

"We thought of that," Danny said. "We're not stupid. We're going to go after the uncles have got back."

"But we've got to look after Pip," Dora said anxiously. "And Uncle Plant said we weren't to go in the Underground today!"

Dennis's grin got even wider. "We're not going to go today. We're going to go tonight, when everyone's in bed. It's a full moon – so if there are any cracks, we'll see the moonlight shining into the tunnels!"

"And there won't be anyone else about," Danny said. "No draglins, no Beanies – nothing!"

Daffodil opened her mouth, and then shut it again. It was just the sort of adventure that she liked best, and she was wishing she'd thought of it.

"It sounds OK," she said grudgingly, and then, "actually, it sounds GREAT!"

Dora felt her stomach turn to ice. "I really don't think it's a good idea," she said, but she knew that nothing she could say would stop her brothers and sister now. She also knew she would have to go with them. It would be far FAR worse imagining what was happening to them if she stayed behind.

CHAPTER FOUR

The little draglins were getting ready for bed when the uncles finally got back home. All three were covered in dust and earth, and looked extremely gloomy.

"Aren't those children in bed yet?" Uncle Damson snapped.

"We were waiting to see—" Daffodil began, but Aunt Plum interrupted her.

"They're just going," she said. "Hurry along, all of you! Clean your teeth, and I'll come and say goodnight in ten minutes!"

There was something in Aunt Plum's voice that made the little draglins scurry away, but as soon as they were out of sight Dennis grabbed Daffodil's arm.

"You or me?" he hissed.

Daffodil knew exactly what he meant. "Me," she whispered, and while Dennis, Danny and Dora went to clean their teeth, she inched her way back to the kitchen door, and put her ear to the keyhole.

"It's bad," she heard Uncle Puddle say. "Very bad indeed. There's another couple of cracks in the roof above the school. We've spent all day moving the desks and the equipment into one of the safe tunnels."

"They should never have built the school in a wabbit burrow in the first place," Uncle Plant growled. "Bound to cause trouble sooner or later."

"We could hear Beanies talking up above us," Uncle Damson added. "Noise must have been coming through the cracks. Never heard 'em before."

"Horrible things, Beanies." Uncle Plant was growling more fiercely than ever. "You know that wabbit hole next to the school? Well, they were stuffing their rubbish down it! Revolting behaviour!"

"Oh dear." Aunt Plum sounded very worried. "So what happens now?"

"We're going back at first light tomorrow to take the school down," Uncle Puddle said, "and just hope we're not too late. If the roof falls in it'd be the first thing a Beanie would see. Everybody's coming out to help – well, everybody our age. Can't risk letting the children anywhere near. MUCH too dangerous."

"That's right." Daffodil heard a crash as Uncle Damson thumped the table. "Make sure you keep 'em in all day, Plum. You know what our lot are like. Always wanting to save the world, and certain they can do it." Uncle Damson sounded almost proud, but Daffodil didn't have time to be astonished. Aunt Plum said, "Oh, goodness! I must go and say goodnight to them. I won't be a minute…"

Daffodil fled.

As soon as Aunt Plum had tucked them in and gone back to the kitchen, Dennis and Danny hurried into Daffodil and Dora's bedroom.

"What did they say?" Dennis asked.

Daffodil reported her findings.

"WOW!" Danny said.

"Fancy leaving us out of it!" Dennis was furious. "We're DEFINITELY going to go now. I KNOW we can find a way to save the school."

"It sounds terribly dangerous," Dora quavered. "Honestly, I don't think we should go..."

"Well, I'M going!" Daffodil told her. "You can stay here if you're scared."

"We'll go as soon as the grown-ups go to bed," Dennis agreed. "Come on, Danny. See you later, Daffy."

Dora, in an agony of indecision, watched them tiptoe out. She turned to Daffodil for help, but Daffodil was already tucked up in her blanket with her eyes shut tight.

"Oh, WHY do we have to have adventures?" Dora thought. "And WHY am I the only one who's scared?"

The door opened a crack, and Danny's head appeared. "You will come, won't you, Dor?" he asked. "I can't cope with Dennis and Daffy on my own."

"I'll come," Dora promised.

CHAPTER FIVE

"Dora! Wake up!" Daffodil was hissing in Dora's ear. "It's time to go!"

Dora, who hadn't slept at all, reluctantly came out from under her blanket. The bedroom, usually pitch black at night, was light enough for her to see her sister's outline, and she knew the moon must be up. She struggled off her sleeping mat, and pulled a sweater over her pyjamas.

"What do you need that for?" Daffodil demanded. "It's summer!"

"It'll still be cold," Dora whispered.

Daffodil snorted as loudly as she dared. Then, side by side, they tiptoed out of their room and found Dennis and Danny waiting for them in the hall.

They could hear Uncle Damson's steady snoring as they crept towards the back door, and odd little squeaks from Aunt Plum, but otherwise the house was wonderfully silent. When the door handle clicked loudly Dora froze, but the snores continued, and the four little draglins made their way outside.

"Right!" Dennis said. "Let's go!" and they moved as quietly as they could into the silver moonlight.

"WOW!" Danny stared around him. "It's almost as bright as day!"

"It's beautiful," Dora said wonderingly.

"Come on!" Daffodil was impatient. "We aren't here to look at—"

"HOOOO! Hoooo hoooo hoooo HOOOO!"

The owl swooped so close that all four draglins jumped, and fled back into the shadows of Under Shed. Dora's heart beat so fast she felt faint, and she clutched at Danny's arm.

"Keep still!" he whispered. "I don't think it saw us – look, it's flying high! There it goes!"

"We'd better run," Dennis said. "It might come back again…"

"What if it sees us?" Dora was trembling all over. "Oh, PLEASE can we go home?"

"No way," Daffodil said. She picked up a dry leaf from the many that the uncles kept piled high to disguise their house. "Cover your head with that, Dor. If the wowl comes back you can freeze, and it won't see you."

"I'll hold it," Danny said. "It's big enough to cover two of us." And before Dora could protest he grabbed her hand. Together they tore across the open ground, the leaf protecting them from the sharp eyes of the owl, and Dennis and Daffodil hurried behind.

Once they were safely inside the Underground they stopped to catch their breath.

"Here we are!" Daffodil was jubilant. "Aren't I clever? Why didn't we ever think of that before? Hey! I bet we could fool even a chat!"

Dora was looking longingly back at Under Shed, and didn't answer. The ivy that covered the old shed walls was gleaming in the moonlight, but even as she gazed a cloud slid across the moon, and the magic was gone.

"Bother," Dennis said. "I was counting on that moon!"

"It'll come out again," Daffodil said. "Come ON!" And she strode into the pitch black tunnel.

"WAIT!" Danny called after her. "Wait for us!" As Daffodil unwillingly came back he went on, "It's really REALLY dark. We ought to hold hands – at least until there's some light. That way we won't lose each other."

"I don't want to hold anyone's hand,"
Dennis grumbled. "And why should Daffy
lead the way? This was my idea!"

"You can lead on the way back,"
Danny said, and Dennis, still muttering,
reluctantly agreed.

CHAPTER SIX

Deep in the tunnel, their eyes gradually grew used to the darkness. The light was very dim, but they could just make out which way to go. The journey was easy to begin with, and Daffodil was inclined to hurry them along, but gradually even she began to slow down.

"It smells different!" she said suddenly, and she was right. Normally the Underground had a faint dampness about it, a comfortable earthy smell, but that was gone. After they had passed the junction that marked the end of their garden there was a dry dustiness in the air, and the ground under their feet became loose and crumbly. It got worse as they drew near to Wabbit's End School, and twice they had to climb over piles of freshly fallen earth.

THUD!

41

"OUCH!" Daffodil squeaked loudly, and stopped.

"What is it?" Dora whispered nervously.

"Don't know," Daffodil answered, "but it's solid. Hang on a moment – OH!" She began to laugh. "It's a desk! This must be where the uncles have stored everything from school!"

Daffodil was right. The tunnel was piled high with tables, desks and chairs, and the four draglins edged their way past with some difficulty.

"Wonder how Uncle Plant got through?" Dennis said, and giggled. Uncle Plant was an extremely substantial draglin, who liked his pies and puddings.

"He'd have got stuck if he'd been in a hurry." Daffodil's voice was muffled. "There's a whole lot more earth ahead blocking the way. Looks as if the tunnel's fallen in. I'm going to see if I can find a way through…"

"Do be careful, Daffy!" Dora was having hideous visions of her sister being buried alive.

"Wait for me!" Dennis pushed his way forward. There was the sound of scraping and scrabbling, and suddenly a clear ray of moonlight shone into the darkness.

Danny, Dora, and the dust-covered Dennis and Daffodil stared in wonder. In front of them was Wabbit's End School, but as they had never seen it before. Instead of being cosily tucked into the side of an old rabbit burrow, warm and safe, it was open to

the skies. Large clods of earth and tufts of withered grass lay in the playground, and a shower of stones had smashed through the roof and into the classroom beneath.

"It looks DREADFUL," Danny said, after a long shocked pause.

Dora began to cry. "Our poor poor school!"

"We're not going to be able to rescue it now," Dennis said. "But we've got to hide it. The first Beanie to walk this way can't help seeing it!"

"And then they'll dig up all the tunnels and we won't have the Underground and I'll never see Violet ever ever ever again!" Dora wailed.

Daffodil snorted. "Never mind weedy Violet. What about our bootball team? Don't be so selfish, Dora."

"Actually," Danny said, and he sounded serious, "I think Violet could be in danger. If they dig up the tunnel they'll probably start on the other side of the school – the tunnel that leads to the peazle fields. There are loads of draglin houses under the fence just across from the Underground entrance…Slump lives there, and Plotter, as well as Violet…"

"Hey! We could block up the entrance!" Daffodil clapped her hands.

"YEAH!" Dennis agreed. "Then the Beanies won't find the tunnel. Come on…" and he ran off across the playground.

"I bet the uncles have already had that idea," Danny thought as he hurried after them. "But maybe we can make it even better."

Dora followed more slowly. Ever since she was tiny she had been told how important it was that Human Beanies NEVER found out about the draglins living in their gardens, or roofs, or allotments, or old garden sheds. To be seen by a Beanie was the most terrible thing in the whole wide world, and would put every draglin's life in danger. Uncle Damson had once told her that if a Beanie ever found her it would keep her in a cage, and never let her out again. Even worse, it would go hunting for other draglins – and Beanies were cunning and clever hunters. Dora shuddered.

What would a Beanie think if it found the school? There was still writing on the blackboard – she could see it through the cracked and dusty window. Wabbits didn't write. Nor did molies, or any other animals she knew of. They would never be safe until all traces of the school had gone. And there was only one way that Dora could think of to make that happen, and her legs almost collapsed under her at the very thought.

FIRE.

A fire would reduce the wooden school to ashes – ashes that would mean nothing to a Beanie.

But how would the fire start?

Dora gulped. She, Danny, Dennis and Daffodil would have to do the most dreadful thing a draglin could ever do.

They'd have to blow smoke...and, even worse, flames.

CHAPTER SEVEN

"**F**LAMES?**"** Daffodil, Dennis and Danny stared at Dora as if she had grown two heads.

"You mean, FIRE?" Dennis said at last. "You want us to set the school on fire?"

Dora nodded. "Don't you see?" she said. "It's the only way."

Daffodil gave Dora a long hard look. "You know what, Dor," she said, "you may be really wimpy sometimes – but at heart you're a HERO."

Even in the moonlight it was clear that Dora was blushing. Daffodil sidestepped Dora's ecstatic hug and took charge.

"Right. Uncle Plant said the Beanies had been putting rubbish in the wabbit hole. If it's paper it'll help the wood burn, and we can stuff some inside the classroom. If you go and look, Dennis,

I'll start breathing fire."

Dennis looked mutinous, but Danny hauled him away. A moment later he came dashing back. "There's LOADS of paper and it smells DISGUSTING," he reported. "And there's an empty sirryget box as well."

Daffodil stopped her heavy breathing. "Brilliant!" she said, her eyes shining. "If we leave the sirryget box nearby, the Beanies'll think that was what started the fire!"

Danny darted off again, and a moment later the strong smell of stale chips filled the air as he came back almost smothered by a sheet of oily newspaper. Dennis was close behind him, staggering under the cigarette packet. "YUCK," Daffodil said. "Aren't Beanies horrible? Now, shove the paper in the classroom. Dora, you can put some round the outside of the school walls as well."

Dennis glared at her. "So we do all the work while you just sit here blowing smoke rings?"

"I'M going to breathe fire just as soon as it's all ready," Daffodil told him.

"But I'm better at smoke than you," Dennis argued.

"No you're NOT!" Daffodil folded her arms and glared at him.

"If we don't hurry up it'll be too late," Danny interrupted. "Look! The moon's disappearing! I think it might be going to rain…"

At once there was a flurry of activity. Dora tore the paper into strips, and filled the classrooms. Danny fetched the remaining pages one by one, and Dennis and Daffodil scrumpled them up and packed them between the school and the burrow wall.

The cigarette packet was arranged behind one of the clods of earth.

*

The four draglins, panting, stood back and admired their work.

"And now I set fire to it!" Daffodil announced.

Dora squeaked, and Daffodil looked at her suspiciously. "You don't think YOU can do it, do you?" she asked.

Dora pointed at the clouds. "I felt a drop of rain!"

"WHAT?" Daffodil looked horrified. "QUICK! Let's all try together!"

Side by side, they began to blow. A few tiny puffs of smoke rose into the air, but there was no sign of any fire.

Danny stopped to cough. "What if we can't do it?"

"We WILL!" Daffodil grabbed his hand. "Come on – we can do it if we try hard enough – I KNOW we can!"

Grimly they went on puffing and blowing. The smoke grew thicker, but there wasn't even the suspicion of a flame. A wind had sprung up, and carried what smoke there was away – but it also blew darker and darker clouds overhead.

"Maybe we're too young," Danny gasped. "Maybe only old draglins can blow fire."

"Rubbish!" Daffodil snapped angrily, and a tiny red spark flew out of her mouth. It faded immediately, but Dennis had seen it.

"WOW!" he said. "Way to go, Daffy!"

Danny stared at Daffodil. "How did she do that?" he wondered – and a thought struck him.

"That's IT! We've got to be ANGRY! Think of all the things that make you MAD…REALLY mad!"

"Being sent to bed early!" Daffodil said. A small shower of sparks flew into the air.

"Being treated like a baby!" Dennis growled, and more sparks scattered.

Danny nodded. "And being told off for something I didn't do!" Again there were sparks, but the wind seized them and whisked them away.

Dora searched her mind for something that made her angry.

"Come ON, Dor!" Daffodil encouraged her. "There must be SOMETHING…"

As Daffodil spoke there was a tiny break in the clouds above, and for a second a shaft of moonlight lit up the abandoned school. Dora gazed at it, and thought of how Pip rushed into nursery shouting "YES! YES!" at the top of his little squeaky voice. She thought of all the times she'd shared secrets with Violet, and how even Dennis and Daffodil zoomed to school when there was a bootball match. She thought of Danny laughing with his friends as he hopped round the playground...and now it was all destroyed, destroyed because of horrible Human Beanies.

Dora shut her eyes and blew...and a clear red flame shot into the darkness.

CHAPTER EIGHT

"Of course, it was my sparks that started it all," Daffodil explained as the four draglins trotted home along the Underground tunnel. "If I hadn't blown sparks Dora would NEVER have been able to start the fire."

Nobody felt it was worth arguing with her. They had watched in awe as the flames had seized hold of the school and soared, scarlet and yellow, up into the sky. There had been a rushing and a roaring, and the CRASH! of falling wood, and then it was all over. Only a heap of glowing ashes showed where the school had once been. The blackened cigarette packet lay a few steps away.

Dora swallowed. Her throat was sore, and she couldn't help feeling guilty. What would the uncles and Aunt Plum say when they found out what had happened?

Danny said, as if he had read her thoughts, "So are we going to say what we've done?"

"YES!" both Daffodil and Dennis shouted at once, but Dora shook her head.

"What do you think, Danny?" Dennis asked.

"I'd say better not," Danny said thoughtfully. "I mean, we've done an awful lot of things we aren't allowed to do."

"But we've saved the day!" Daffodil protested. "We're HEROES!"

"That's right," Dennis agreed.

"Why don't we go home and back to bed, and see what's going on in the morning?" Danny suggested. "We could wait until the uncles come back from seeing the school—"

"And then we could go, TA-DAAAA! WE did that!" Daffodil beamed.

As the draglins tiptoed across the open space between the Underground and their front door, the rain began. Huge drops bounced on the hard earth, and by the time they reached Under Shed all four of them were soaked.

"Better take our shoes off," Dora whispered as they crept inside.

"OK." Dennis yawned, and followed Danny towards their bedroom. "See you in the morning!"

CHAPTER NINE

Dennis, Danny, Daffodil and Dora all overslept. They were woken by the extraordinary sound of Uncle Puddle, Uncle Plant and Uncle Damson laughing loud jolly laughs as they crashed in through Under Shed front door.

"Plum! PLUM!" they yelled. "We've been to Wabbit's End – and you'll never guess what! The school's vanished...burnt to a cinder! And we've blocked the tunnels, and it's POURING with rain, so we'll be safe as houses now!"

The four small draglins flew into the hallway to find Uncle Damson swinging Aunt Plum round and round.

"YIPPEE!" she shouted. "YIPPEEEEEE!"

"Do you hear that, children?" Uncle Plant was grinning from ear to ear. "You won't need to worry any more!"

Daffodil coughed loudly, and stepped forward. "Actually," she began, "we weren't worrying. You see – " she spread her arms wide to include her brothers and sister – "it was US who did it. WE set fire to the school! At least – " Daffodil looked at Dora, who was wriggling uncomfortably – "Dora did!"

There was the longest silence, and then Uncle Puddle began to laugh. "HA!" he chortled. "Good joke, Daffodil! For a moment there I almost believed you!"

Uncle Damson frowned. "This is NOT a joking matter," he said. "This is LYING! And a terrible lie at that!"

Uncle Plant rubbed his chin thoughtfully. "I wonder…"

"Just a minute." Aunt Plum was studying her nephews and nieces. "They do smell of smoke," she said. "And there were wet footprints on the carpet early this morning."

"Sorry, Aunt Plum," Dora said automatically.

"We used the paper from the wabbit hole!" Dennis couldn't bear the doubt on Uncle Damson's face any longer. "We

67

stuffed it in the classroom and all round, and then we set fire to it!"

There was another silence.

"And HOW, exactly, did you set fire to it?" Uncle Damson asked at last, his face an ominous purple.

Dora burst into tears. "It was me, Uncle Damson, and I know I'm a bad BAD draglin, and I promise I'll never ever EVER do it again – but the Beanies would have caught us and I WON'T let them do it, I won't, I WON'T! And you can punish me as much as you like and I didn't mean to do it but someone HAD to!" And she threw herself into Aunt Plum's arms, wailing loudly.

Uncle Plant began to clap, and Uncle Puddle shouted, "Three cheers for Dora, Danny, Daffodil and Dennis!"

Uncle Damson looked over their heads at Aunt Plum.

"They have saved us, Damson," she said quietly. "You'd never have got the school out of sight in time, however hard you tried."

"No," Uncle Damson said, very slowly. "No, we wouldn't. And there's another thing. Not one of us thought of burning it down, even though we grown ups always think we're cleverer than the children."

He stood up straight, and put his hands on his hips. "Puddle, Plant – you're right. Three cheers for our nephews and nieces – and a special celebration breakfast!"

"HURRAH!
HURRAH!
HURRAH!"

HAVE YOU READ ALL THE DRAGLINS BOOKS?

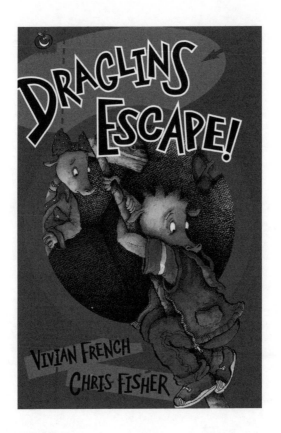

Daffodil, Dora, Dennis and Danny
can't believe they are moving to the great
Outdoors! How will they get down from
Under Roof? And will they get to see the
scary chats and dawgs they've
heard so much about?

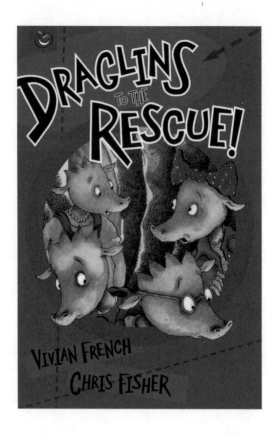

Daffodil, Dora, Dennis and Danny
have moved Outdoors, but their things are
trapped Under Roof! Dennis has a PLAN
to rescue them... But will the gigantic
Human Beanies get in the way?

Wowling has been heard near the draglins'
home in Under Shed! Daffodil, Dora, Dennis
and Danny come face to face with a scary chat
for the first time ever – are four little
draglins a match for terrible
teeth and sharp claws?

What will draglin school in the great
Outdoors be like? Daffodil, Dora, Dennis
and Danny don't know what to expect,
but their classmate Peg does.
She wants to be boss!

Here comes a fierce crow with a big
beak – is this the end of Dennis? It was meant
to be a splendid day out from school, but
he's got himself lost in a field. Will Daffodil,
Dora and Danny find him in time?

Human Beanies are dangerous, especially
when they're blowing smoke. Now there's
a fire in Under Shed, and the flames are
spreading! Can Daffodil, Dora, Dennis
and Danny save their home?

Daffodil, Dora, Dennis and Danny are
off to visit Great Grandmother Attica, but it's
a scary journey. Can they save themselves, let
alone a little ducklet lost on the
edge of the Great Wetness?

by Vivian French
illustrated by Chris Fisher

All priced at £8.99.

Draglins books are available from all good bookshops,
or can be ordered direct from the publisher:
Orchard Books, PO BOX 29, Douglas IM99 1BQ.
Credit card orders please telephone 01624 836000
or fax 01624 837033 or visit our website:
www.orchardbooks.co.uk
or e-mail: bookshop@enterprise.net for details.

To order please quote title, author and ISBN
and your full name and address.
Cheques and postal orders should be made
payable to 'Bookpost plc.'

Postage and packing is FREE within the UK
(overseas customers should add £2.00 per book).

Prices and availability are subject to change.